GOOD NIGHT FAIRY STORIES

ARORA'S

Rs.99/-

CONTENTS

THIEF
OF
BAGDAD

Once upon a time, a young orphan boy named Hassan lived in the ancient city of Bagdad. He had no parents and kept himself alive by stealing from the rich merchants who travelled to the city each day to sell their wares. Every night he would sleep under the walls of the mosque that overshadowed the city.

Day after day, Hassan lived in this way, and sometimes the Caliph's men, called by the merchants, would see him and try to catch him. They would chase him through the city crying, "Stop thief!" but, of course, Hassan ran faster to escape from them. They never caught him.

When he felt safe, he would empty his pockets of all he had stolen. There would be loaves, fruits and often a bottle of wine. One day, leaning against a tree, Hassan ate some bread and fruit, then took the cork from an oldish-looking bottle. There was a faint pop and a hissing noise. As he bent forward to sniff the contents, to his amazement, vapour from the bottle curled out and rose up, bigger and bigger, higher and higher into the sky!

Writhing this way and that, the vapour suddenly turned into an enormous man towering above him. Poor Hassan shook with fear as he looked up at the huge figure, for he knew not whether the giant was good or evil.

Smiling, the giant looked down at the trembling boy and said, "Don't be afraid for I am your slave. Whatever you command, I will obey." He held out his hand.

Hassan knew then, that it was no dream.

When Hassan had got over his surprise and fright he said, "Take me to the Caliph's Palace, so that I may see the beautiful Princess."

"Climb on my back, little master, and hold on tight," said the slave and soon they were flying over the rooftops of the city. How exciting it was!

Hassan held on tightly for he was still just a little bit scared.

The city looked so tiny far below him and the slave seemed to fly very fast. He had to pinch himself to make sure that he was not imagining it all. Only a few minutes ago he had been a poor orphan boy being chased out of the city and now here he was flying!

The slave began to slow down and circled gently round the Caliph's Palace, the towers shining in the evening light. They glided down to a big, open window.

"There," whispered the slave and lowered Hassan to the floor. Looking round in wonder he found himself in a fine bedroom with rich hangings, a tiger-skin rug on the floor, a golden bed and, wonder of wonders, there was the Princess.

She lay fast asleep in her beautiful bed, her soft, black hair hanging in a cloud round her pillow.

At once Hassan fell in love with her; straightaway, he knew he loved her dearly. Looking down at his poor clothes, he knew he must hide or he might wake and frighten her. But as he turned, he bumped into a small table, and the slight sound woke the sleeping girl.

"Don't be afraid, I just wanted to see you," he said, "my name is Hassan. I will not hurt you."

"Go quickly, or the guards will find you," she said.

"Farewell, lovely Princess, I shall not forget you." And Hassan climbed out of the window into the city darkness.

The Princess turned over in bed and thought of Hassan. He had not frightened her and she wondered about him. She was engaged to marry Prince Genghis of the Red Plume, but she did not love him. She was frightened of him for he was cruel and scheming. He was already plotting the downfall of her father once he married the Princess, for he wanted his rich kingdom very badly.

The Caliph knew his child was unhappy and told Prince Genghis that she must decide the wedding date, but

the Prince was very angry and demanded they marry at the next full moon. He told the Princess that unless she agreed he would send his army, which was very strong, to fight her father's small force, and take over her peace-loving country.

The Princess was very unhappy for she knew she loved Hassan. In despair, she told her father she could not marry Prince Genghis, whatever happened.

"Father, I love Hassan," she wept, "I hate Prince Genghis. He is cruel and wicked. I cannot marry him."

"Who is Hassan?" asked the Caliph, "is he a prince?"

"He is a poor little thief from Bagdad," she replied.

"A thief!" cried the Caliph.

"I met him the other day, but I will marry him, for, in spite of everything, I know he is good and honest."

Prince Genghis, who had been listening outside the door, heard the Princess's words and burst in.

"You want to marry a thief!" he cried. "I'll find him and hang him, the rogue! How dare you prefer a guttersnipe to a Prince of my greatness," he roared.

"No, stop, please," begged the Princess, "don't hurt him."

"Hurt him!" sneered Prince Genghis, "I'll kill him."

He laughed, an evil, menacing sound as he turned to go from the room.

Suddenly, a strong wind blew through the Palace, fluttering the curtains, banging the windows, ruffling the rich wall hangings.

Out of nowhere, Hassan appeared wearing fine silks and satins and smiling at the Princess who ran to greet him. He looked very handsome in his rich clothes. Everyone else gasped in amazement, for behind Hassan stood the tallest giant they had ever seen. It was his slave of the bottle.

"I am Hassan," the boy said,
"I have come to ask for
the hand of the Princess
in marriage."
And he walked up
to the Caliph's throne.

"This man is a thief,"
cried Prince Genghis,
"seize him," he told the guards.

As the guards moved to obey, the Prince snatched up
a sword himself and rushed to attack Hassan.

Swiftly, the giant lifted up the struggling Prince,
opened a window, and, holding him high in the air, flung
him up into the sky. He was never seen again.

The Caliph realised how wicked Prince Genghis had been and threw his arms round his beloved daughter, telling her she and Hassan could be married—even if he was a thief, though he doubted so great a man could be one.

Hassan fell on his knees and thanked the Caliph then he held the Princess in his arms.

The giant smiled. Hassan looked at him and thanked him for all he had done. "Is there anything I can do for you in return?" he asked. "Can I give you anything?"

"My freedom," the giant replied.

"You have it," said Hassan, "go and do good all over the world, my friend. I shall never forget you."

With a wave of his hand, the giant disappeared in a cloud.

"He's gone," said Hassan sadly as he gazed out of the window at the rising cloud.

"Never mind, he brought us together", reminded the Princess, and that made them both smile again.

The Caliph put the wedding preparations in hand straightaway and there was great rejoicing throughout the land.

Hassan and his Princess lived happily ever after, but he often thought of his faithful slave and wondered how he was helping! Whenever he opened a bottle, he always took special care, just in case he might find another slave inside.

THE WOLF AND THE SEVEN KIDS

"Listen, my children", said the old nanny goat to her seven lively kids, "I have to go quickly into the woods to get food. Be very good, do not fight with each other and, above all, do not open the door to anyone, it might be that wicked wolf." She gave each one a kiss and went on her way.

But as you will probably have guessed, the wolf had waited for her to leave, because young, plump kids were his favourite food. He crept quietly up to the closed door and knocked, and said in a deep voice, "Dear little children, open the door, I am your mother and have brought you something nice."

The kids were very sensible and cautious, however. "We are not that stupid to let you in, you nasty wolf," they shouted, "our mother has a soft, high voice and not a deep voice like yours." Then the wolf swallowed a whole lot of chalk in order to make his voice really high pitched. "Open up, you dear little children," he squeaked, and knocked at the front door once again, "I am your mother." But the kids looked through the gap of the door and saw a pair of black feet. "No, no," they shouted in disgust, "our mother has feet as white as snow. Stay outside you wicked wolf!"

The crafty wolf then made his way to the baker and

asked him to cover his paws with flour. The baker thought it seemed rather an odd thing to ask, but he took one look at the wolf's sharp teeth, and did as he was bid.

The wolf returned to the house and knocked at the front door for the third time and when the kids saw his white paws, they called out, "Oh, yes, this is our mother!" and they cheerfully opened the door. But the poor little kids got such a fright when they saw the wicked wolf pushing his way into the house! Whatever would happen to them now?

They quickly looked for somewhere to hide. One crept under the bed,
another one hid behind the curtain, another
hid behind the fire screen, one took refuge under
the soup terrine, and one even crawled into the stovepipe.

But there was no getting away from him. The wolf caught them all and swallowed them up. Only the youngest kid was saved because it had hidden in the grandfather clock, and the wolf did not think of looking in there.

Soon afterwards the old nanny goat arrived back home. She had brought a big basket full of delicious grasses and herbs. "It's good to be home", she thought, "and my children will be so happy with these wonderful titbits."

But oh horror, the front door was left wide open...! the little kids had all disappeared...!

Inside the house, the room was in a terrible mess. Everything was untidy. The chairs had been thrown over and the soup terrine was smashed. The old goat could hardly believe her eyes. There was absolute silence and nothing moved, and not a single kid was in sight. The tears ran down the nanny goat's face.

She sobbed and cried, "Oh, my poor children, if only you had listened to your mother! Now you have all been eaten by the wicked wolf!"

Just then a squeaky little voice called from the grandfather clock, "Mother, open up, I am still alive!" The mother was so happy that she could at least hug one of her children! But...

"Listen," the little kid suddenly called out, "Who is snoring so loudly? I think the wolf is lying down in the garden and is fast asleep."

"Indeed, it is him," called the nanny goat. "Quickly, child, fetch my big scissors! Who knows, perhaps your brothers and sisters might still be alive. we must try to save them!" The nanny goat ran as fast as she could into the garden and—**snip, snip**—she cut open the wolf's stomach. The kids crawled out happily one after the other!

How happy everybody was. They all hugged and kissed each other. "Now, children," said the mother, "everyone of you fetch a heavy stone and put it into the wolf's stomach!" The kids did this as quickly as they could. Then the nanny goat skilfully stitched up his stomach, so that he should not feel a thing and just grunted a bit in his sleep. The kids laughed and hid with their mother in the house.

At last the wolf woke up, yawned and stretched and started to run around. Because he was very thirsty, so he bent over the well in order to have a drink. The weight of the heavy stones pulled him down into the deep well and he splashed down, right to the bottom. The kids had been watching from the window and **then** they pranced into the garden, feeling very happy and relieved. The wicked wolf was lying in the well and was no longer a danger.

The kids and their mother held each other by the paws and danced around the well singing, "Hurray, the wolf is dead ! He will not hurt us anymore. Now we can all live happily ever after !"

HANSEL AND GRETEL

On the edge of a forest lived a woodcutter with his two children. Their names were Hansel and Gretel.

For a long time the children were very happy. They would go off with their father in the early morning and stay near him while he worked. They kept themselves busy gathering berries and nuts and mushrooms and would also pick bunches of wild flowers.

But everything changed when their father married again, for their stepmother turned out to be a cruel woman who hated the children.

"There are too many mouths to feed," she complained to her husband. "What a quantity of food these children eat, and us, so poor! I tell you, we must get rid of them."

This made the woodcutter very uneasy.

Nevertheless, the stepmother nagged him until one night, when Hansel lay awake in bed, he heard his father agreed to take the children into the forest and leave them there.

Next morning, before the grown ups were awake, Hansel crept outside and filled his pockets with pebbles. When they had some breakfast, their father took them into the forest, farther than ever before. "Wait for me here," he said.

He lit a fire of brushwood to keep them warm and then sadly turned his back on them.

When it grew dark, Hansel said: "Father will not come back, but I have left a trail of pebbles and we can find our own way."

As soon as the moon came up, the little white pebbles shone like stars and led them all the way home to their father's cottage.

No one else could have been more surprised than the stepmother.

That night, Hansel heard her saying to their father: "I will not have it! You must take them deeper into the forest this time."

Sadly over-ruled by his wife, the woodcutter took his children even farther into the forest. Unhappily, Hansel had not been able to gather pebbles, for the stepmother had taken care to lock the cottage door. "Do not worry," whispered Hansel to Gretel. "I have crumbled the bread I got for breakfast and have dropped it on the way."

But there was no trail, for the birds had flown down and eaten every crumb. Gretel began to cry, but Hansel said: "Look! There is smoke rising above the trees. It may be a woodman's hut."

The children hurried through the trees and soon found themselves in a little clearing. There stood the strangest little house they had ever seen. Its walls were made of ginger-bread and its roof was made of cake, and all the windows were made of barley sugar.

Soon they were nibbling away at the little house for they were very hungry. Hansel broke off a piece of the roof and Gretel broke off a piece of the window.

Then out popped a little old woman. "Come in, my dears!" she said in a friendly voice.

The old woman made a delicious meal for them, and when they had eaten their fill, she led them upstairs where there were two little beds. What a kind old woman she seemed to be! But dear! she was really a most wicked witch.

Next morning when Gretel woke up, Hansel was gone. "Where is my brother?" she asked the old woman, but the reply she got was:

"Fetch some firewood! The oven must be kept hot."

· When she was fetching the wood, Gretel found Hansel locked in the chicken-house.

"You must find a way to save me," cried Hansel, "for she plans to cook and eat me!"

And this was exactly what she meant to do, and she had chosen Hansel because he was bigger and plumper.

All day long Gretel carried wood and the witch piled it on to the fire until the little kitchen was as hot as it could be.

Every time she passed the chicken-house, Gretel would whisper to Hansel; "Do not worry, Hansel, I will think of a way to save you!"

"Surely the oven must be hot enough now," said the witch impatiently. "Put your head in and tell me if it is hot enough," she said to Gretel.

"Not yet," said Gretel.

The witch put on more wood and told Gretel to test it again. "Is it hot enough now?" she asked.

"Not yet," said Gretel.

"Silly goose!" said the witch. "It **must** be hot enough! I will test it myself." And she put her head in the oven.

Quick as lightning, Gretel gave the witch a push that sent her headlong into the oven. Gretel slammed the door and fixed the bolt.

Then she ran out to Hansel.

Gretel broke the lock on the chicken-house door and she and Hansel ran back to the cottage. "What will you give me if I let you out?" said Hansel to the witch in the oven.

"I will give you my magic stick," said the witch. "It will obey your command and turn anything, it touches, into nice things to eat. Take it! I don't care! Only please let me out!"

"And do you promise to be good from now on and eat no more poor children?" asked Hansel.

"Yes, yes, I promise!" wailed the witch.

Hansel snatched up the stick and Gretel unlatched the oven door, and out stepped the old woman, rather hot and bothered but smiling. From that day on she was a good, kind old woman and loved the children dearly.

She cared for Hansel and Gretel like a loving grandmother and they lived with her in the magic cottage.

Hansel only had to say to the magic stick: "Bring my father here!" and they would hear the woodcutter knocking at the chocolate door of the gingerbread cottage and his kind voice saying:

"How are you,
my dears?"

RAPUNZEL

There was once, long ago, a beautiful girl called Rapunzel who had been stolen away by a witch when she was just a baby. She had lived all her life in a tall tower where the witch kept her a prisoner. The tower had neither door nor staircase, but only a little window, high up in the wall.

The witch would come to visit her everyday.

When the witch wanted to get into the tower, she would call out in her rasping voice:

"Rapunzel, Rapunzel, let down your hair."

Rapunzel had long golden hair, and when she heard the witch call she would fasten her hair to a hook outside the window and let the long braid fall to the ground. Then the witch would climb up and squeeze through the little window.

As you can imagine, it was very lonely for Rapunzel in the tower, and often she would sing to pass,the time, away.

One day, a Prince was riding through the forest and heard her sad song. He fell in love with the sweet voice and longed to know who lived in the tower.

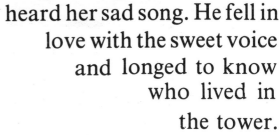

As he watched, the witch appeared and he saw how she climbed up to the little window.

As soon as she had gone away he too called:
"Rapunzel, Rapunzel, let down your hair."
And he climbed up the golden braid.

Rapunzel was startled
to see the Prince, for in all her
life she had known no one but the witch.

Everyday, the young Prince came to the tower to visit Rapunzel.

How handsome the young man was, and how Rapunzel longed to leave the tower and go with him out into the world!

Day by day, they plotted together how to escape. Rapunzel was so happy, thinking about how she might escape, that one day, when the witch was visiting the tower, she said a foolish thing.

"How heavy you are, Mother Witch, compared to the young prince," she said.

"Wicked girl!" screamed the witch. "So you have been deceiving me!" "You were my treasure and I thought I had hidden you away from all the world. No fate is too awful for such wickedness!"

From the folds of her cloak, the witch brought out an enormous pair of scissors and cut off Rapunzel's beautiful hair. She spirited Rapunzel to the deepest part of the forest where she would be left to die. Then she waited for the Prince.

When he called, "Rapunzel!" the witch let down the golden braid and the Prince climbed up.

"Ah!" she cried, "the beautiful bird is gone and the cat that has taken her away will soon scratch your eyes out!"

The king's son was beside himself with grief. He jumped from the tower, fell into the branches of a

thornbush. Needle-sharp
thorns pierced his
eyes, and he
was blind.

Leading his great white horse by the bridle, he
wandered through the forest, mourning his lost love.
Days, months and years slipped by and still the Prince
lived in the forest. Everyday he moved on, going deeper
and deeper into the forest and called as he went:
"Rapunzel!
Rapunzel!"
But there was never an answering call; only the sad
echo of his voice among the trees.
Then one morning, after he had lain all night under
the shelter of an ancient trees, he heard the sweet, sad song

he remembered so well. He knew it was she.
    "Rapunzel!"
    he called.
    "Rapunzel!"
    Rapunzel knew his voice and came running to meet her Prince.

    Weeping with joy, she threw her arms about his neck. Two of her tears fell on his eyes and magically his sight returned.
    Happy beyond words, the Prince lifted Rapunzel on to his white horse and rode with her to his own kingdom. There they lived long and contentedly together and were never again troubled by the wicked witch.

THE FAIRYFOOT

A long time ago, in a faraway part of the country, and quite hidden by a thick forest, there was a town called Stumpinghame. No one knew how far the forest

stretched—and no one had ever tried to find out. First, because it was known to be inhabited by the fairies, and second, because the people of Stumpinghame were no travellers. Man, woman and child had feet so large and

heavy that they were able to walk only
the shortest distances.

Stumpinghame had a King and his name was
Stiffstep. His Queen, Hammerheel, was a great beauty.
Her majesty's shoes were almost as large as fishing-boats
and her six children took after her. All went well until the
birth of their seventh—a son.

For a long time, nobody about the palace could
understand what was the matter. The ladies-in-waiting
looked so astonished, and the King so vexed; but
at last it was whispered that the seventh child
had been born with such miserably small
feet that they resembled nothing
ever heard of,
except the feet
of the fairies.

So ashamed were they that they sent the young Prince to be brought up by the shepherd. The King and Queen had given him fourteen names, beginning with Augustus, but the country people could not remember so many; so they called him Fairyfoot.

So Fairyfoot grew up in the shepherd's cottage and all agreed that he would have been handsome but for his small feet. Nevertheless, he learned to walk—and to run and jump, which was quite unknown. But the old people thought him unlucky and sent him out everyday to watch sheep on a wild pasture on the edge of the forest.

One summer day, as he watched the sheep, a robin, chased by a hawk, flew down beside him. He covered it with his old velvet cap and the hawk flew away. Instead of the robin, from under the cap stepped out a little man.

"Thank you," he said, "My name is Robin Goodfellow. Now, can I do something for you?" Fairyfoot noticed that the little man's feet were as small as his own.

'No one will play with me because my feet are not

large enough", said Fairyfoot. "Then play with us," said the little man.

He led Fairyfoot along a mossy path until they came to a meadow where the moon shone as bright as day. A crowd of little people were dancing round a clear, crystal well. Under tall rose trees there were tables with dishes of honey and carved wooden flagons filled with clear red wine. The little man handed one of the flagons to Fairyfoot.

The boy had never before tasted such a drink. As soon as it touched his lips he forgot all his unhappiness and danced with the little people till the moon was low in the sky. Then the little man led him back to the shepherd's cottage.

All that summer, Fairyfoot went into the forest and he was never tired or sleepy. But one night, Fairyfoot was in such a hurry to join the dance, he did not drink the clear, red wine. What hard work it was to keep pace ! At last he was glad to sit down behind a mossy oak. He fell asleep, and only awoke at the sound of voices close beside him.

Two little ladies were having a conversation. "What handsome feet he has!" said one. "Yes," said the other. "They are just like the feet of Princess Maybloom before she washed them in the Growing Well. Now no doctor can make them small again. Only the water of the Fair Fountain can do that and only I and the nightingales know where that is."

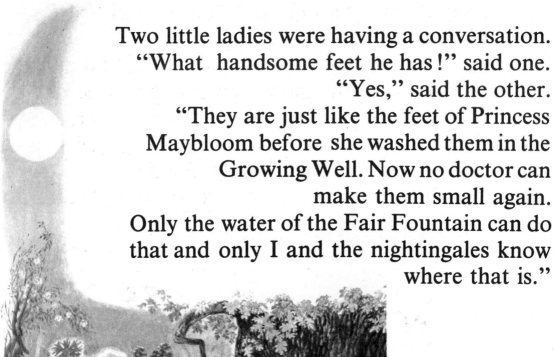

"You will surely tell the Princess?"

"Not I! If it were known, wouldn't it bring crowds of those great coarse creatures who must surely long to have small feet!"

Next day, Fairyfoot was so tired that he fell asleep and the flock strayed away. He awoke with the shepherd's angry shout and made off into the forest, not stopping till he reached the banks of a stream. He followed it for many hours to a grove where nightingales sang.

"What boy is that?" said one, "and how did he find his way here?"

"How silly you are!" said another. "He only had to follow the ground-ivy which grows from the smallest gate of the King's garden to the root of this tree."

Fairyfoot thought he would follow the ground-ivy and see the Princess Maybloom. It was a long journey, but it led him at last to the smallest gate in the King's garden. As the boy climbed over, a dappled fawn frisked by and a sad voice said:

"Come back, my fawn!
I cannot run and
play with you now
that my feet have
grown so heavy!"

Fairyfoot knew it must be the Princess.

"Princess", he said, "I know of a fountain that can make your feet as small as ever they were. But it must be kept secret or the fairies will be offended."

The Princess danced with joy in spite of her large feet.

So with two maids, the King's chamberlain,
and the pet fawn, Princess Maybloom
set out with Fairyfoot to follow
the ground-ivy.

At last they
reached the magic
grove.

The moment
the Princess's
feet touched the water
they grew smaller, and when she had washed them three times they were as small as Fairyfoot's.

"Oh", sighed Fairyfoot, "if there had been a well in all the world to make my feet large, my father and mother would not have sent me to live among the shepherds!"

"As you have shown me the Fair Fountain, I will show you the Growing Well", said the Princess.

There was a great joy in the palace because Princess Maybloom's feet were small again. Soon, Fairyfoot and Princess Maybloom were married, and between the two royal families things worked out very nicely. When the young couple went to visit Stumpinghame they washed their feet in the Growing Well, and on the way back they stopped at the Fair Fountain.

THE BABES IN THE WOOD

Once upon a time, two children lived in a big house on the borders of a wood.

Their parents, who loved them very dearly, were rich enough to buy them everything they wished for, and all day long they played in the beautiful garden.

But one sad day, their father and mother died and the sister and brother were left alone.

The children had an uncle whom they had never seen. He lived far away across the seas; but as soon as he learned of the death of his brother, the children's father, he hurried to their home. He knew that now their father was dead, the children would have all his money, and the uncle also knew that if he could get rid of the children all this money would be his.

The more he thought about this money the more he longed for it. And then a dreadful thought came into his head.

He would kill the children and take the money. So he hired two robbers, and paid them to take the children to a lonely spot in the wood and kill them.

One morning, the robbers crept into the garden where the children were playing and took them away. The men led them out into the wood till they came to a deserted spot. They had come a long way and the children were glad to rest. They sat down on the trunk of a tree while the robbers moved away and spoke in low voices.

"Why kill them?" said one. "Let's leave them, and perhaps someone may find them and give them shelter."

The little girl crept closer to her brother. Then the other robber came and spoke to them.

"Stay here while we go to find food and shelter for the night," he said gruffly.

But it was a lie.

They went away, and the children were left all alone in the wood

They had come too far to be able to find the way back and so they wandered on, hoping to find shelter. For a time they were happy walking among the ferns and

wild flowers, but soon the sun went down and a great stillness came over the wood.

At last the children sat down under an oak tree and fell asleep.

The shy squirrels with their long bushy tails glanced wonderingly at them. And the gentle wind shook the leaves so that they fell, making a cloak to cover them.

When morning came, all the creatures rushed about finding food for the children. The squirrels brought nuts, the birds brought berries, and Robin told them which one would be safe for children to eat. Even the owl went back to his house in the tree and brought them each a tasty morsel. Old Grandpa Fieldmouse wasn't best pleased.

Then Robin said: "I shall fly off and find someone who will take care of them."

"How can you tell them that the children are here?" asked the wise owl.

"Leave that to me," said Robin and he flew down and tweaked a button from the little boy's coat.

Then Squirrel frisked down the tree.

He nibbled the little girl's hair ribbon with his sharp teeth till he had cut right through. Then he handed the tiny piece to the Robin.

Soon Robin was ready to set out. The blue ribbon was tied neatly around his throat, and in his beak he carried the bright, shiny button. He flew straight to a cottage on the edge of the wood. The old woman who lived there was his friend, for she never forgot to put out crumbs for him. He perched on a branch by the cottage door and sang his loudest.

"Bless me!" said the old woman.
"There's my friend,
the little Robin!"

Robin flew down and dropped the bright, shiny button at her feet.

"Bless me!" said the old woman when she recognised the button from her little grandson's coat.

And when she glanced back at the little Robin she recognised the blue ribbon her little granddaughter's cap.

Robin flew a little way off and sang again and the old

woman put on her shawl and followed him. Robin led her to the heart of the wood.

"Bless me!" cried the old woman when she saw her two little grandchildren.

"Oh, Grannie!" said the little boy. "We had such a horrid dream!"

"Bless me!" said the old woman.
"That's all over now."

THE SNOW CHILD

One winter day, two children asked their mother if they might go out and play in the new-fallen snow. The little girl was called Violet; and although it was not her real name, her little brother was always called Peony because his cheeks were like two red peony roses.

The little garden in front of the house was divided from the street by a white fence.

The trees and shrubs were leafless now, and their twigs were covered with snow.

"Yes, you may go out and play in the snow," said their mother, and out they went with a hop, skip, and jump.

"Peony," said Violet, "let's make a figure out of snow—a little snow-girl to run about and play with us all winter."

"Oh, yes!" cried Peony.

"But Mamma must not make her come into the warm parlour," said Violet.

The children began to make a snow-figure. In fact, it seemed not so much to be made by them, as to grow under their hands.

"Now," said Violet, "we must have some little shining bits of ice to make the brightness of her eyes."

"Mamma!" called Peony. "Look out and see what a nice little girl we are making!"

The mother put down her sewing and looked out of the window. Through the dazzle of the sun on the snow, she could see the snow-child, and thought there never was a snow-figure so cleverly made.

She went back to her seat, and the children worked on in the garden.

"What a nice playmate she will be for us all winter long!" said Violet.

"Oh, yes!" cried Peony. "And she shall sit down close by me and drink some of my warm milk!"

"Oh, no, Peony!" said Violet. "That will not do at all. Warm milk will not be good for our little snow-sister. Little snow-people, like her, eat nothing but icicles."

Just then there came a breeze sweeping through the garden and rattling the parlour windows.

It sounded so wintry cold that the mother was about to tap on the window-pane to bring the two children in, when they both cried out to her. "Mamma! We have finished our little snow-sister and she is running about the garden with us!"

The sun had now gone down and the mother could see the garden quite plainly. Besides Violet and Peony, there was a small figure of a girl, dressed all in white, playing with the children!

She called Violet to her and whispered: "Violet, my dear, what is this child's name?

Does she live near us?"

"Why, Mamma," laughed Violet, "it's our little snow-sister!"

Just then, a flock of snow-birds
came down. They flew at
once to the snow-child,
fluttering about her head.

While the mother wondered what to think and what
to do, the garden-gate was thrown open
and the father of Violet and Peony
appeared. He soon noticed
the little white stranger.

"What little girl is this?"
he asked. "Her
mother must be
crazy to let her go
out in this bitter weather
wearing only a flimsy white dress."

"I do not know," said his wife.
"Some neighbour's
child, I think."

"Father, do you not see how it is?" said Violet. "This is our snow-figure which Peony and I have made because we wanted a playmate."

"Nonsense, child!" said their father. "Do not talk about making live figures out of snow. This little stranger must not stay out in the cold a moment longer. We will bring her into the parlour and give her a supper of warm bread and milk. I will go out and ask about a lost child."

"Father!" cried Violet. "Do not make her come into the hot room. She cannot live unless she breathes the cold air!"

"Nonsense!" said the father. "Run indoors."

The little white creature fled backwards, but the father chased her into a corner where she stood, glistening like a star.

Violet's and Peony's eyes filled with tears when the little white figure was led into the warm parlour. The father placed her right in front of the stove. "Give her some warm milk," said he.

Then out he went, but he had hardly reached the gate when the screams of Violet and Peony brought him back.

"Father, you would bring her in," cried the children, "and now our little snow-sister is thawed!" And the father, not understanding such things, said: "What a quantity of snow the children have brought in on their feet!"

THE SELFISH GIANT

Every afternoon, the children
used to go and play in
the Giant's garden. It was
a large garden with twelve
peach trees that in spring time broke
out into delicate blossoms and in the
autumn bore rich fruit.

KEEP
OUT

The Giant had been away
for seven years—but one

day he came back. He saw the children playing in the garden.

"What are you doing here?" he said in a loud, gruff voice.

The children ran away.

"My own garden is my own garden," said the Giant.

So he built a high wall all round it and put up a notice saying, 'Keep out'.

He was a very selfish Giant. Now the children had no place to play.

The spring came, but in the garden of the selfish Giant it was still winter. The trees did not blossom and the flowers did not bloom because they missed the children. The only ones who were pleased were Snow and Frost.

They brought the
North Wind and he roared
all day about the garden.
Then the Hail came and rattled on the
roof of the Giant's castle.

"I cannot understand why the Spring is so late," said the selfish Giant.

But Spring never came, nor Summer. Autumn brought fruit to every other garden but not to the Giant's. "He is too selfish," she said.

One morning, the Giant was lying awake in bed when he heard some lovely music. It was really only a little linnet singing outside the window, but the garden had been silent for so long, the sound delighted him.

He went to the window and looked out. Through a hole in the wall the children had crept in. The trees were smothered in blossom, except for one which was still covered in frost.

A little boy stood there crying.
He was too small to
climb up. The Giant
went out to the garden
and lifted him.

"How selfish
I have been!"
he said.

"Now I know
why the Spring
did not come
here.

I will knock down the wall, and my garden shall be
the children's playground for ever and ever."

The little boy stretched out his two arms and flung
them round the Giant's neck. The other children came
running when they saw the Giant was not wicked any
more. "It is your garden now, little children," said the

Giant, and he took a great axe
and knocked down the
wall. When the people were
going to market,
they saw the
Giant playing with
the children in the garden.

In the evening, the children
came to say good night. "Where is
the little boy?" asked the Giant. "He has gone away,"
answered the children. Everyday the children came to
play, but the little boy never came back. "Oh, I would
like to see him!" the Giant sighed.

Years went by and the Giant grew very old. One winter morning he looked out and saw that one tree was in blossom and beneath it stood the little boy he loved. He hurried out, crying: "You have come back, my child!"

and the child smiled and said: "Today you shall come with me to my garden, which is paradise."

THE REAL PRINCESS

There was once a Prince who wished to marry a princess, but he said she must be a real princess.

He travelled all over the world in the hope of finding her, but now one thing, now another, seemed not quite right about the ladies he met.
Sadly he returned to the palace.

One evening, during a fearful storm, with thunder and lightning, and rain pouring down in torrents, there was a violent knocking at the palace door. The old King went himself to open it and found a princess standing outside. She was in a sorry state, with the rain-water dripping from her hair; but she said she was a real princess. "We shall soon see!" said the old Queen-mother, and she went to the guest bedroom and took off the covers. She put three little dried peas on the bedstead and then laid twenty mattresses one upon the other over the three peas, and put twenty feather-beds over the mattresses.

On this the Princess was to pass the night. Next morning, the Queen asked how she had slept.

"Oh, very badly," she replied. "I have scarcely closed my eyes the whole night through. I had something hard under me and it hurt me so much that I am black and blue all over."

Since she had been able to feel three little peas through twenty mattresses and twenty feather-beds, she must surely be a lady of great delicacy. Indeed, a real princess!

PRINCE ZEYN

There was once a King of Balsora who was rich, and good, and loved by the people he ruled. He had one son whose name was Zeyn.

When this son was born, the wise men studied the stars and said they could see a wonderful future for him.

The young prince grew up and was taught everything that princes ought to know; but when he was still young, his father became ill. Knowing that he was going to die, he sent for Prince Zeyn.

"Soon you will be king," he said. "Try to be a good king. Do not listen to those who always praise you, and try to find out the real truth before you punish anyone."

But after the old King died Zeyn's only thought was pleasure. At last his mother reminded him of his father's words and Zeyn felt ashamed. One night he had a dream that an old man was standing by his bed.

"Oh, Zeyn," he said, "joy comes after sorrow, happiness after sadness. Dig your father's room. There you will find treasure." Next morning, Zeyn dug until his axe struck against stone. This he lifted eagerly and under it was a marble staircase. In the chamber below he found ten large jars full of gold, and in the second chamber, nine pedestals.

On all the pedestals but one stood shining diamond statues. On this pedestal was written: 'The ninth statue is the most beautiful. Go to Cairo and find the slave, Mobarec.'

Zeyn set off at once and found Mobarec who was now a rich merchant. When Mobarec was sure that this was indeed the son of his old master, he set out with Zeyn in the quest of the ninth statue.

After travelling many days they came to the country where the statue was. Mobarec signalled to a little boat and soon they were on the Island of the Genii.

In a flash of lightning, the King of the Genii appeared before them.

"It was I who gave the King, your father, the eight statues. The ninth I will give you on one condition. You must find a maiden who has never, in her life, spoken an angry word or thought of anger. Bring her to wait upon my Queen and I will give you the statue."

Zeyn agreed, but he knew it would be a hard task. "How shall I know this maiden?", he asked.

"Here is a magic mirror," replied the King. "Only the right maiden will be able to see her face in it."

So Mobarec and Prince Zeyn went out into the world again to find a perfect maiden.

First they went back to Cairo, but amongst all the beautiful girls there, no one could see her own face in the mirror.

Next they went to Bagdad where they met an old man named Muezin who said he knew the most perfect maiden in the world.

Muezin took Prince Zeyn to see her, and when her father heard that he was the son of the King of Balsora, he was very pleased to see him, and at once allowed his daughter to look into the magic mirror. The moment she did so, she saw her own lovely face in the shining glass.

Zeyn had found the perfect maiden that he sought.

Now there was only one way to take her from her father and that was to marry her. But Zeyn loved her already, He found it very hard to keep his promise and to take her back to the King of the Genii. The King was pleased and said: "You will find the ninth statue in its place when you return."

Prince Zeyn went sadly home, thinking he would rather have the perfect maiden than the ninth statue. He walked with his mother down the marble staircase and stared at the ninth statue.

It was not made of diamonds.
It was the perfect maiden whom he loved.

THE FROG PRINCE

Once upon a time, in a beautiful palace in a far away country, lived a young princess who was the only child of her parents, the King and Queen.

Her favourite present was a golden ball the King had given her on her birthday. Everyday, she played by the lime tree in the palace garden, tossing and catching the golden ball.

One day, as she threw it high in the air for the pleasure of seeing it glisten in the sunlight, it splashed into the lily pond. Of course, being made of solid gold, it sank at once to the bottom.

The Princess was in tears. Then a frog hopped out of the water on to a lily pad.

"Princess," he croaked. "Shall I fetch the golden ball?"

"Please ! Please !" said the Princess.

"What will you give me for a reward?" asked the frog.

"Oh, I would give anything to have my golden ball back," said the Princess. "Even my gold ring set with pearls."

"I do not care for your gold ring set with pearls," said the frog, "but let me be your companion. Let me eat from your crystal plate, drink from your silver goblet, and sleep on your silken pillow."

"I promise," said the Princess impatiently. "What a silly frog !" she thought.

With a splash, the frog was off the lily pad and diving deep to the bottom of the pool. Presently there was another splash as the frog returned with the golden ball in his mouth.

The frog tossed the golden ball on to the grass.

As soon as the Princess had got back her treasure she forgot all about the frog and ran back to the palace. She raced across the lawn, leaving the frog hop, hopping, a long way behind.

"Foolish old frog!" she said. "He can go back and splash in his pool. What do I care!"

That night, the Princess sat at supper with the King and Queen and the ladies and gentlemen of the court. Tall silver candlesticks glittered on the table and soft music drifted down from the musicians' gallery. There was a quiet murmur of conversation and the rattle of silver spoons as the servants helped the guests from the silver dishes.

During a short lull in the music, the Princess thought she could hear a soft, thudding little noise on the marble staircase.

Everyone listened and it seemed to come again. Then there was another sound, hop, hop, hop, just outside the door, and a soft little tap, tap, tap, on the panel, and a croaky voice saying:

**"Lovely Princess,
Open to me!"**

The Princess went slowly across the room. She opened the door a little way, then shut it quickly.

"It's only an ugly old frog," she said.

"A frog?" exclaimed the King.

And before; he could say another word there was another tap on the door and the frog's voice croaked again:

"Don't you remember
The promise you made,
When you lost your toy
In the lime tree's shade?"

The ladies of the court gasped and the gentlemen stared in amazement.

"What is he talking about?" asked the King, becoming impatient and a little bit cross.

He looked at the Princess and the Princess turned quite pink.

She had to explain all about how she lost her golden ball, and how the frog brought it back to her on one condition, and how she had given her promise.

The Princess looked sulkily at her father.

"I will never agree to have him as a companion. I do hate him so. Please, Father, have someone take him back to the garden."

The King looked severely at the Princess.

"You are a royal Princess," he said, "and whatever promise you made, you must keep. Even a promise to an ugly frog. Now, open the door and let him come in."

The Princess looked sulkier still, but she went and opened the door and the frog came in, hop, hop, across the carpet, up to the table, and came to rest beside the Princess's chair.

The Princess sat down in her palace and looked with disgust at the ugly green frog.

"I can't reach the table," he croaked. "Lift me up, Princess!"

Pouting, the Princess set the ugly frog on the linen table-cloth where he sat blinking his sad, small eyes at the candle light.

"Give me my supper," he croaked.

"Fetch a plate," said the Princess to one of the servants.

"But have you forgotten?" asked the frog. "You promised I should eat small from your own crystal plate."

The King looked sternly at the Princess, so she pushed her beautiful crystal plate nearer the ugly frog, who ate some of her supper.

After that, she could not eat a bite, but she picked up her silver goblet to sip some wine.

"Give me a drink," croaked the frog.

"Bring a saucer of water," said the Princess to the servant.

"Have you forgotten?" asked the frog.

"You promised I should drink from your own silver goblet."

So the poor Princess passed her silver goblet to the frog who took several sips of wine.

Then he sighed, looked round with his sad, beady eyes, and croaked:

"Where is your bed? I am tired."

The Princess stamped her foot angrily.

"Take him upstairs to rest," said the King. "He helped you when you were distressed, now you must keep all the promises you made to him."

The Princess dared not disobey the King.

"Hop upstairs and I will find you a room," she said to the frog.

The frog closed his eyes sleepily.

"I cannot hop further," he said. "You must carry me."

Shuddering, the Princess picked him up by a foreleg and carried him upstairs.

She set him down in the doorway of an empty room.

"Don't you remember your promise? I am to sleep on your silken pillow," said the frog.

But she did not put him on her silken pillow. She put him in the darkest corner of her room. She was so tired that she fell asleep as soon as she got into bed. She had only been asleep for a few minutes when a soft little sound woke her. Hop, hop, hop. There sat the ugly frog by the side of her bed.

"Your promise, Princess!" he croaked.

The Princess flew into a temper. Leaping out of bed, she picked him up and threw him on to the silken pillow. "You ugly creature!" she screamed. "Why do you torment me?"

She picked him up and with all her might, threw him out of the window. She looked out—and there in the garden below, stood a handsome prince.

"Princess," he said,
"you have broken
the spell that has
changed me into
a frog."

The Princess's heart melted at the very sound of his voice. And so, would you believe it ! The Princess married the Frog Prince, and drove away with him into his own country.

PRINCE AHMED AND THE PRINCESS

Long, long ago in old Persia there lived a rich Sultan named Omar and his lovely daughter, the Princess Nurina, who was the apple of his eye.

She was so beautiful that many Princes from the neighbouring kingdoms sought her hand in marriage, but she refused them all. They spent their time in idleness, eating and drinking and courting her favours, but she found them very dull and refused to marry any of those who tried to win her. She longed for a man with courage and skill, not a **court** flatterer who was a coward at heart. Her father, the Sultan, understood and shared her feelings.

One day, Ahmed, a Prince from a far off land, lost his way while out hunting and came to the Sultan's Palace for rest and refreshment.

He soon learned of Princess Nurina and her loveliness which he wanted to see for himself.

"May I see your daughter?" he asked the Sultan the next day. "No one may see my daughter unless he can prove himself a man of strength and determination and one who is worthy of her," the Sultan replied.

"Won't you even let me just look at her?" begged the Prince.

The Sultan remained firm and Prince Ahmed gathered his retinue together and rode sorrowfully on his way.

But he was now determined to find a way of proving his worthiness to win the hand of the Princess, although he knew many had tried and failed.

As Prince Ahmed rode on he remembered, how, many years ago at his father's Court, he had talked with an aged soothsayer who had told him of strange things:

"In the years to come you will seek a beautiful bride, but to win her you must first find three things. You will need a magic telescope which can see everything, even through walls, a magic carpet to fly you wherever you wish and a magic bow and arrow which will never fail your target."

"But where will I find such things?" asked the Prince.

"Seek for the telescope in a remote city, in the house of a merchant, hidden in an old trunk. Then journey on to a lonely village where you will discover a small carpet, green in colour with a red and yellow pattern. When you have these things, you will see the bow and arrow."

Then Ahmed knew what he must do. He set out.

After journeying for many miles with much fruitless searching, Prince Ahmed reached an old, remote city whose very walls seemed to hold the secrets of the past.

This must be the place, he thought, and looked for the house of the merchant.

The merchant's son told him his father had an old telescope stored somewhere, given to him by a magician who said a young man would come for it one day. He promised to find it for the Prince. "Come back in three days," he said, "and I will have it ready for you."

In three days Ahmed returned and was shown a very old telescope, painted a dull red. This must be the one, he thought excitedly, and paid the merchant two gold pieces.

The merchant also had a bow for sale but somehow the Prince knew it was not the magic one.

"Next find the carpet", thought Ahmed and, looking through the telescope, he saw a tiny village in the far distance. Night was falling, but he knew his search for the carpet had ended.

A carpet dealer said to him that he had the very one he wanted—small, green, with an unusual red and yellow pattern on it, which would carry him where he pleased. The deal was made, the Prince and his servant quickly climbed on to the carpet and commanded it to fly. In a moment, they were airborne, riding high above the desert.

Looking through the telescope, Ahmed saw an archer with a large bow slung across his shoulders. Instinctively he knew this was the magic one and quickly descended to buy it.

Airborne once more, Ahmed flew towards the city
and as he approached the Sultan's Palace,
he saw one of the Viziers pacing up
and down looking very worried.

"Descend," he ordered the carpet, and approached the Vizier.

"Why are you so unhappy?" he asked.

"It is the Princess Nurina," the Vizier replied, "she is ill, pining away, but no one can help her."

"What is wrong?" asked Ahmed in concern.

"An Evil Spirit has cast a spell on her which cannot be broken," said the Vizier, "everyone has tried."

"Let me try," begged Ahmed, "I think I know the secret of how to do it."

"Well, it can do no harm," said the Vizier, "come with me."

"I have three magic things," Ahmed told him, "a telescope with which I can see anything, even through a wall; a magic carpet which brought me here and a bow and, arrow which never misses its target."

Ahmed looked through his telescope and immediately saw the Evil Spirit standing on a high turret overlooking the Palace, his gaze fixed on the Princess. The Spirit, who was very cunning, instinctively knew he was being spied on and looked around to see who was looking at him.

At that moment, the Princess, released from his evil gaze, began to stir from her long sleep and opened her eyes. The Sultan called everyone to her bedside.

"Nurina wakes! She is well!"
He clapped his hands
in delight.
"Thanks to Allah."

Seeing Prince Ahmed, the Evil Spirit flew into a great rage. With a terrifying look he started to descend from the turret towards Prince Ahmed.

Hurriedly, the Prince dropped the telescope and picked up the bow and arrow. Fixing the arrow into his bow he shot it high into the air. The arrow first flew on a straight course but then, suddenly, it turned in the direction of the Evil Spirit.

Just then, the Sultan and Nurina came out into the courtyard, looking for the stranger, their Vizier had told them about. It was a strange sight that met their eyes.

"Ah!" screamed the Evil Spirit as the arrow struck him between the eyes, transfixing him to a stone parapet. With an ear-splitting shriek, he was converted in a ball of fire and was never seen again.

The Sultan and his daughter had watched in amazement as the arrow changed its course to kill the Evil Spirit.

"It must be magic!" they cried. "Who can the archer be?"

Just then, Prince Ahmed entered the Palace, bow in hand, and asked to see the Sultan. The courtiers gathered round him offering their congratulations to this wonderful archer who got rid them of the Evil Spirit.

The Sultan stepped forward. He recognised the Prince as the man who had wished to see the Princess on his earlier visit.

"A welcome return!" cried Omar, "and many thanks for saving my daughter. You have earned the privilege of meeting her."

At first glance, Princess Nurina and Prince Ahmed knew their dreams were fulfilled. Turning to her father, she said, "I would like to marry this Prince who has proved himself so brave and resourceful."

The Sultan was delighted and straightway a grand wedding was planned.

People from far and wide came to join in the wedding celebrations and everyone was happy that their Princess was marrying to a Prince so fine.

In all the excitement, the magic telescope, the carpet and the bow and arrow were forgotten and no one knew what happened to them. Nor did anyone really care now that all was well in the land!

THE TAILOR'S HELPERS

There was once a tailor who had become so poor, through no fault of his own, that one day he only had enough cloth left to make just one jacket. He cut out the cloth that evening so that he could sew the jacket together the next morning. Then he went up to bed, said his prayers and fell asleep.

The next morning when he sat down to start work, he noticed that the cut out cloth had been made into a complete jacket. He was amazed and could not imagine how it could have happened. He held the jacket up to the light to take a closer look at it. It had been so well sewn that every single stitch was perfect.

Soon afterwards a customer came to buy the jacket and because he liked it so much he paid a higher price for it than usual, then the tailor was able to buy cloth for two more jackets. He cut out the material that night, and the next morning he intended to start work sewing the jackets together, after a refreshing night's sleep.

But the next morning, when he sat down at his table, the cut out cloth had once again mysteriously been made into jackets. Soon two customers came along and bought both the jackets.

The tailor then had enough money to buy material for four new jackets. The next morning, after cutting out the cloth the night before, all the jackets were completed when the tailor sat down at his table.

This went on
for a long time.
Whatever the
tailor cut
out in the evening,
he would find the
material made up
into jackets the next morning.
Soon he was making a good
living for himself and his wife,
and he became a wealthy
man.

One evening, just before Christmas, he said to his wife, "Let's stay up tonight and discover who's been doing all this work." She agreed and they both hid in the corner of the workshop behind the curtains. They watched closely and as the clock struck midnight some little gnomes appeared, sat down at the table and began to sew the cloth together to make the jackets.

The tailor and his wife were amazed and could not believe their eyes. The gnomes did not stop working until all the jackets had been completed. Then they ran off.

The next morning the tailor's wife said, "Those little gnomes have made us very wealthy, we really should repay them somehow or other. I've been thinking and I've had an idea. I suggest that I make them some new clothes—little shirts, jackets, waistcoats, trousers and socks.

Their clothes looked rather ragged, so I'll even make them a little pair of shoes each." The tailor replied, "Oh, what a lovely idea!" and his wife immediately set to work.

They put out the presents for the gnomes that night and hid in the corner to see what the little men would do with the clothes. Would they be pleased with them, they wondered?

At midnight the gnomes appeared and were about to start work on the cut out cloth when they noticed the little sets of clothes. At first they were amazed and then overjoyed! Quickly, they put the clothes on and they cried,   "Aren't we smart now!
Why should we carry on
being tailor's helpers?"

They laughed and jumped and capered about and finally they danced out of the door and were never seen again. But the tailor and his wife lived happily and prospered all their lives.

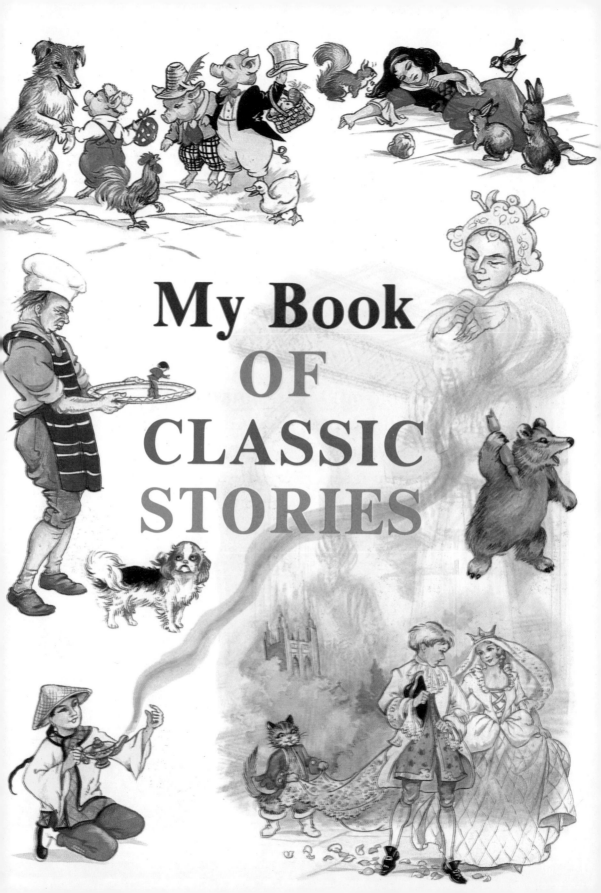

My Book
OF
CLASSIC
STORIES

CHILDREN'S ILLUSTRATED DICTIONARY

WITH GENERAL INFORMATION

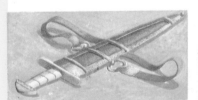

ARORA'S